The Black Cat

ALLAN AHLBERG · ANDRÉ AMSTUTZ

GREENWILLOW BOOKS, NEW YORK

Text copyright © 1990 by Allan Ahlberg. Illustrations copyright © 1990 by André Amstutz. First published in Great Britain in 1990 by William Heinemann Ltd, a division of Reed International Books. First published in the United States in 1990 by Greenwillow Books. All rights reserved. No part of this book may be reproduced or utilized in any form or by any means, electronic or mechanical, including photocopying, recording, or by any information storage and retrieval system, without permission in writing from the Publisher, Greenwillow Books, a division of William Morrow & Company, Inc., 105 Madison Avenue, New York, NY 10016.   First American Edition   10 9 8 7 6 5 4 3 2 1
Printed in Great Britain by
Cambus Litho, East Kilbride

Library of Congress Cataloging-in-Publication Data
Ahlberg, Allan.   The black cat.
Summary: A little black cat watches the antics
of three skeletons sledding in the snow.
[1. Skeleton—Fiction.   2. Snow—Fiction.
3. Cats—Fiction]   I. Amstutz, André, ill.
II. Title.   PZ7.A2688B1   1990   [E]
90-2886   ISBN 0-688-09903-3.
ISBN 0-688-09904-1 (lib. bdg.)

In a dark dark town,
on a cold cold night,
under a starry starry sky,
down a slippery slippery slope,
on a bumpety bumpety sled . . .

a little skeleton is sliding . . .
and sliding . . .
and crashing – wallop!

The little skeleton
loses a leg in the snow.
A white leg in snow
is hard to find.
A black cat in snow
is easy to find.
What is <u>she</u> doing here?

The little skeleton and the big skeleton
go to the boneyard
to get a new leg
for the little skeleton.

They play around with the bones
for a while . . .
and go home to bed.

Then . . .
in the dark dark town,
on <u>another</u> cold cold night,
under a starry starry sky,
down a slippery slippery slope,
on a bumpety bumpety sled . . .

two skeletons are sliding . . .
and sliding . . .
and sliding . . .
and crashing – bang!
WALLOP!
This time the big skeleton
loses a leg in the snow.

A white leg in snow
is hard to find.
A black cat is easy.
Is she still here?
I wonder why.

The big skeleton
and the little skeleton
go to the boneyard
to get a new leg
for the big skeleton.

They play around again with the bones
and go home to bed.

Then . . .
in the dark town,
on the <u>next</u> night,
under a starry sky,
with a moon, too,
down a slippery slope,
in the frosty air,
on a bumpety sled . . .

<u>three</u> skeletons are sliding . . .
and sliding . . .
and shouting . . .
and barking!
And banging! Wallop! CRASH!

This time the big skeleton
and the little skeleton
lose the dog skeleton.
A white dog in snow
is hard to find.
But a noisy dog is easy to find.
So is a black cat!

The dog skeleton chases the cat.
Now we know –
that's what she is here for!

The dog chases the cat
up and down
the dark dark hill,
in and out
of the dark dark boneyard,

round and round
the dark dark streets
and down and down
to the dark dark cellar.

But a black cat in a cellar
is very hard to find.
Can <u>you</u> see her?

Well, the dog skeleton couldn't,
and the little skeleton couldn't,
and the big skeleton didn't even try.
So off they went – at last – to bed.

Meanwhile . . .
in the same town,
on the same night,
under the same sky,
down the same slope,
a bumpety sled is sliding . . .

with a black cat on it.